Disney

Oz

THE GREAT AND POWERFUL

THE LAND OF OZ

Adapted by Scott Peterson and Michael Siglain
Based on the screenplay by Mitchell Kapner and
David Lindsay-Abaire
based on the books of L. Frank Baum

Executive Producers Grant Curtis, Palak Patel,
Philip Steuer, Josh Donen
Produced by Joe Roth
Screen Story by Mitchell Kapner
Screenplay by Mitchell Kapner and
David Lindsay-Abaire
Directed by Sam Raimi

Disney PRESS
New York

Printed in the United States of America

First Edition

1 3 5 7 9 10 8 6 4 2

G658-7729-4-12349

ISBN 978-1-4231-7093-8

SUSTAINABLE
FORESTRY
INITIATIVE

Certified Chain of Custody
Promoting Sustainable Forestry

www.sfiprogram.org
SFI-01415

The SFI label applies to the text stock

For more Disney Press fun, visit www.disneybooks.com.

For more Oz fun, visit www.disney.com/thewizard.

This is the story of Oz.

Oscar was a magician from
Kansas.

People called him Oz for short.

He was a very good magician.

He was not a very good man.

Oz was not a bad man.

He was just a selfish man.

He often made people angry.

He often had to get away quickly.

One day, Oz got away in a hot-air balloon.

Oz's balloon got caught in a tornado.

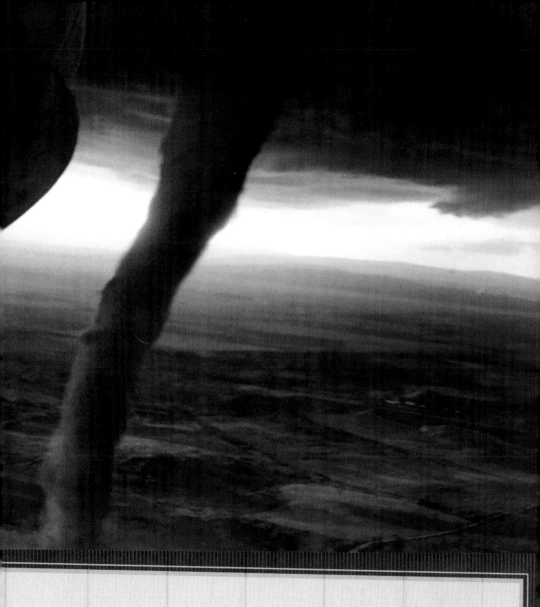

The tornado carried him far away.

It carried Oz to the Land of Oz.

The Land of Oz was so beautiful.

Oz the magician had never seen anything like it.

He had also never seen so many strange creatures.

Oz met a monkey with wings.

The monkey's name was Finley.

Finley could fly and talk.

Oz and Finley became friends.

Oz also met Theodora.

Theodora was a witch.

She was very pretty.

She thought Oz was a wizard.

So he pretended to be a wizard.

Theodora showed Oz her home.

It was called the Emerald City.

The entire city was green.

Oz was treated like a king.

Theodora had a big sister.

Her name was Evanora.

Evanora was also a witch.

Evanora told Oz he could be king.

But first Oz had to do something.

He had to defeat the Wicked Witch.

Oz wasn't happy about this.

He wasn't really a wizard.

He couldn't defeat any witch.

He didn't even want to try.

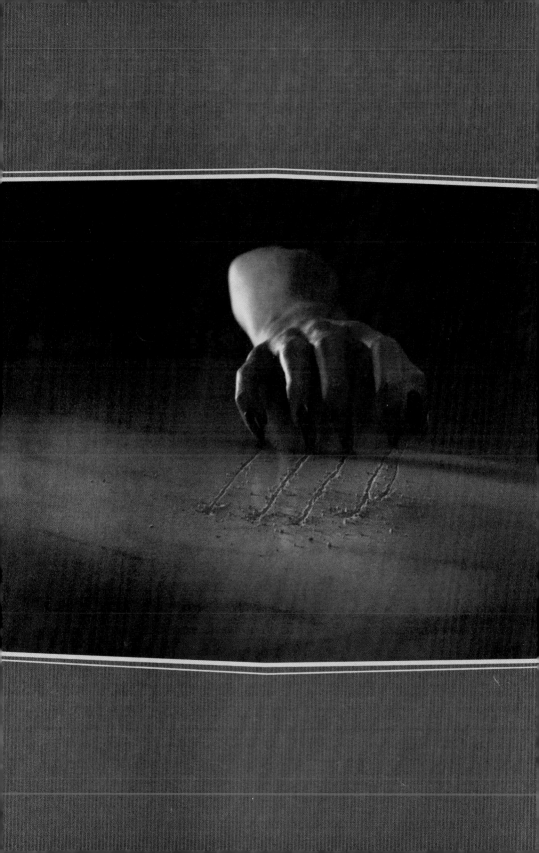

But Oz really wanted to be king.

So he went to find the Wicked
Witch.

Finley went with him.

Together they met China Girl.

Then they found the Witch.

The Witch was Glinda.

Oz realized she was not wicked.

Glinda was a good witch.

Evanora had tricked him.

Evanora was really the bad Witch.

She also tricked her sister.

Evanora changed her sister, and made her evil.

She was now a wicked witch, too.

The sisters wanted to rule the Land of Oz.

Oz and Glinda became a team.

They wanted to help the people
of Oz.

They used Oz's magic tricks.

They fooled the Witches.

Oz and Glinda saved the land
of Oz.

Everyone was very happy.

The Munchkins were happiest
of all.

They sang and danced.

Everyone sang and danced
with them.

Oz could have gone back to Kansas.

But he stayed in the Land of Oz.

He and Glinda would watch over it.

Together.